Sleepy Book

Sleepy Book

by Charlotte Zolotow

pictures by Stefano Vitale

HarperCollins*Publishers*

Bears
    sleep
        in
    their
        dark
            caves
        the long
            winter
        through

pigeons

sleep

in

a row

pressing

against

each other

for

warmth

fish sleep

among

the green

water ferns

with

their eyes

and mouths

wide

open

moths

    sleep

with wings

        folded together

they look like

    little

white leaves

on walls

    and windows

and screens

horses

sleep

standing up

in fields

and stalls

their tails

switching

to keep away

the flies

seals

sleep

with

their

flippers

flat

against

blocks of

ice

the snowy

crane

sleeps

standing

on one long

leg

like

a flower

on its

stem

crickets

　　sleep in

　the long

　　meadow grass

　　　and look

　like the grass

　　itself—

they are

　　so

　still

turtles

sleep inside

their

shells

and no one

would know

a turtle

was there

caterpillars

sleep in

their

silky

cocoons

spiders
    when
they sleep
        are like
            small
        ink spots
        in the
            middle of
        their
lacy webs

kittens

sleep

in the warmest

place

they can find—

curled up

in a basket or

stretched out

purring

in the sun

dogs

sleep

under beds

or in boxes

or on rugs

near

someone

they

love

but little boys

        and girls,

when the night

    comes

and the wind

      whispers gently

         in the trees

and the stars

     sparkle and shine,

sleep

     warm under

their blankets

     in their

       beds.

to my mother

Sleepy Book
Text copyright © 1958 by Charlotte Zolotow
Text copyright © renewed 1986 by Charlotte Zolotow
Illustrations copyright © 2001 by Stefano Vitale
Printed in the U.S.A. All rights reserved.
www.harperchildrens.com

Library of Congress Cataloging-in-Publication Data
Zolotow, Charlotte.
Sleepy book / by Charlotte Zolotow ; illustrations by Stefano Vitale.
p.   cm.
Originally published: 1958
ISBN 0-06-027873-0 — ISBN 0-06-027874-9 (lib. bdg.)
1. Sleep behavior in animals—Juvenile literature.   [1. Animals—Sleep behavior.
2. Animals—Habits and behavior.   3. Sleep.]   I. Vitale, Stefano ill.   II. Title.
QL755.3 .Z66   2001
591.5'19—dc21
00-057252

Typography by Pamela Berry
2   3   4   5   6   7   8   9   10
❖
Newly Illustrated Edition